W9-CDA-613

For my husband and our herd of little elephants—
my home is with you.
—K. F.

For Kirstin, who loves elephants,
& for all the adventurers who go beyond their creature comforts.
—L. S.

Text copyright © 2021 by Katie Frawley
Illustrations copyright © 2021 by Laurie Stansfield
All rights reserved.

No part of this book may be reproduced, or stored in a retrieval system, or transmitted in any form or by any means, electronic, mechanical, photocopying, recording, or otherwise, without express written permission of the publisher.

Published by Two Lions, New York

www.apub.com

Amazon, the Amazon logo, and Two Lions are trademarks of Amazon.com, Inc., or its affiliates.

ISBN-13: 9781542008549 (hardcover)
ISBN-10: 1542008549 (hardcover)

The illustrations are rendered in digital media.

Book design by AndWorld Design
Printed in China

First Edition

10 9 8 7 6 5 4 3 2 1

two lions

Tabitha and FRITZ TRADE PLACES

Written by Katie Frawley

Illustrated by Laurie Stansfield

www.Lair-BNB.com

ATTENTION: Pampered suburban cat seeks wild world traveler for exciting exchange. You'll experience:

FIRST-CLASS COMFORT!

FIVE-STAR SERVICE!

FANCY, FRILLY FUN!

Contact Tabitha the cat today!

Dear Fritz,

Wonderful! This coddled kitty can't wait for her rain forest adventure. I'm off to pack. Keep in touch!

Cheers,
Tabitha

P.S. I hope your birthday is as sweet as can be!

Dear Tabitha,

When I arrived, an adorable little human hugged me hello. She took me to a watering hole. I really made a splash!

Rested and relaxed,
Fritz

P.S. Watch out for Rocky. He does **NOT** play well with others.

Dear Fritz,

Little human? You must mean Claudia. If she tries to play Beauty Parlor, run. Her makeovers always rub my fur the wrong way.

Your herd gave me a warm welcome and showed me around. Scratching posts! Swatting toys! Even my own personal litter box!

I'm making tons of friends. The neighborhood is buzzing! I haven't seen Rocky, but I did discover family in the area. It's like we're **TWINS**!

Feeling fierce,
Tabitha

Dear Tabitha,

Yesterday I tasted the local cuisine. I think I chipped a tusk on my doughnut. Lucky for me, your house has a room *just* for food. I don't miss grazing one bit!

Grand and gourmet,
Fritz

P.S. Claudia sure spends a lot of time getting ready. At home, I usually go for a quick roll in the mud.

Dear Fritz,

I'm glad you like my food! Your herd, unfortunately, does **NOT**. Oh well. More mouse pizza for me!

Last night my relatives invited me over for dinner. I really impressed them with my killer instincts.

Primal and pouncing,
Tabitha

P.S. The quick mud roll was not my cup of tea.

Dear Tabitha,

Today was just awful. First, I got in trouble while sightseeing at the museum. Then, to make myself feel better, I gave myself a dust bath. Now everyone's mad at me. What did I do wrong?

Stumped,
Fritz

P.S. I heard Claudia talking about a party. She must want to surprise me for my birthday. I could use some cheering up.

Dear Fritz,

I had a tough day too.
I got stuck between a hippo and a hard place.

And you were right about Rocky. He's worse than my neighbor's schnauzer!

Fearing for my fur,
Tabitha

P.S. Enjoy your party! Claudia throws a wild one.

HAPPY BIRTHDAY!

Dear Tabitha,

My birthday party was a disaster! Nobody sang to me, all the little humans tried to eat my cake, and the pony didn't like me **AT ALL**.

Last year my herd surprised me with a trip to a waterfall. **THAT** was a happy birthday.

Singing the blues,
Fritz

Dear Fritz,

I know just the waterfall you mean. Your herd dragged me there and insisted I take a dip. I need a nap . . . and a steaming bowl of Claudia's catnip tea. I wish she were here . . . or I were there.

Lost in longing,
Tabitha

Dear Tabitha,

What do you say we cut this swap short? City life is too wild for me.

Itching for a switch,
Fritz

Dear Fritz,

You read my mind! The rain forest has its perks, but there's no place like home. Safe travels!

Homeward bound,
Tabitha

Dear Tabitha,

Home at last! I sent you a little thank-you gift.
Hint: I hope you're ready for a family reunion!

Contented,
Fritz

Dear Fritz,

How thoughtful! I'm packing your present now.
Hint: Sharing is caring!

I have an idea for you: How about we take a trip **TOGETHER**?!
Which would you like more . . . snow or sunshine?

Talk soon!

Preening and purring,
Tabitha

P.S. The doorbell just rang! Could your present have
arrived already?